ustice on Horseback

Agnes M. Hagen

New Readers Press

For Janet and Carole, who helped.

Justice on Horseback
ISBN 1-56853-049-8
Copyright © 2001
New Readers Press
U.S. Publishing Division of Laubach Literacy International
Box 131, Syracuse, New York 13210-0131

Printed in the United States of America
9 8 7 6 5 4 3 2 1

President and Publisher: Richard T. La Pointe, Ph.D.
Executive Director of Publishing: Dennis E. Cook
**Director of Acquisitions and
   Development:** Christina Jagger
Content Editor: Terrie Lipke
Copy Editor: Judi Lauber
Production Director: Deborah Christiansen
Cover Design: Kimbrly Koennecke
Cover Illustration: Luciana Mallozzi
Designer: Kimbrly Koennecke
Production Specialist: Heather Witt

All proceeds from the sale of New Readers Press
materials support literacy programs in the United States
and worldwide.

Chapter 1

Her hair was gold, above blue eyes that were quick to smile. Her soft lips touched his. Jack Sloan held Ann in his arms. He didn't ever want to let her go.

There was a time when Jack loved only his wife, Molly. But Molly died over a year ago. Ann was a comfort to Jack. She loved his young son, Tommy. When the three of them were together, Jack felt as if they were a real family.

Tonight, he would ask Ann to marry him. If only the words would come. Jack was a brave sheriff. But when it came to women, the fearless sheriff was shy.

Jack started slowly. "It sure is a pretty night. Look at all those stars. They, uh, remind me of your eyes, Ann. And the moon is so . . . Ann, will you marry me?" The words slipped out so fast that they surprised even him.

Ann looked up with tears in her eyes. "Jack Sloan, you know that I love you. Of course I will be your wife!" She put her arms around him, and they kissed. They both knew that their love would last forever.

On a warm spring evening, Ann and Jack stood before the parson. Ann wore a beautiful white dress, and she had flowers in her hair. After the couple said their *I do*s, Tommy handed Jack a gold ring. Jack slowly put the ring on Ann's finger. All of the people in the church began to sing.

Outside, Jack's old friend Nate shot off a gun. With a bang, the party began. Ann, Jack, Tommy, and their friends went outside too.

They enjoyed good food and drink. It was a lovely night. They danced until stars shone in the sky.

Nobody saw the man on the black horse. He watched the party from a hill at the edge of town. Putting his head down, he lit a cigarette. The match light showed lines on his face. It was a face that had seen many days on the trail.

Chapter 2

At last, the party ended. Ann picked up Tommy. He had fallen asleep on a blanket. The ride home was happy. Their wagon was covered with flowers and ribbons. Ann leaned against Jack. They didn't see the bent rider on his black horse. He rode slowly, just far enough away not to be noticed.

The next few days were filled with joy. Ann and Jack spoke of hopes and dreams. They wanted to build a bigger cabin so they could have many children. Tommy, who was almost five, had been asking for a brother or sister.

Jack wanted to plant more land and buy cattle and horses. He was thinking of hiring someone to help.

Ann wanted to start a sewing club. She and her friends always had sewing to do. It would be much more fun to do it together.

The Sloan home was full of joy. But nearby, a lone horseman watched from his hideout.

Chapter 3

A week later, Ann stood in the doorway, watching the rain. She was surprised to see a stranger on a black horse.

"Howdy, ma'am," he said as he came near. He put his hand to his hat and got off his horse. "Is this the home of Jack Sloan?"

"Yes, sir, it is," replied Ann.

"And as of last week," she added proudly, "I am Mrs. Sloan." Ann felt there was something familiar about him. His clothes were old and worn. He seemed alone and sad. She wanted to help him.

The stranger looked at Ann. He saw how happy and pretty she was. Jack was lucky, he thought.

"Tell Jack that someone is here to see him," he said.

"He's gone to town," Ann said. "But he'll be back soon. Come in and dry off. I'll pour some hot coffee. We must be quiet, though. Tommy, our boy, is still sleeping."

Ann felt at ease with the

stranger. She talked to him about Jack, Molly, and Tommy. Jack came back from town. As he opened the cabin door, he stopped and stared at the man drinking coffee.

"Dan?" he said as he walked in. "Is it really you, Dan?"

"Jack," said the stranger. "It's been a long time. I've been in a cave for days working up the nerve to face you. Can we forget our differences and be brothers again? You're the only family I've got."

Jack walked over to his brother. He put his arms around the man. "It's been too long, Dan, too long."

Chapter 4

Seeing Jack and Dan hug, Ann could tell they looked alike. That must be why she felt so close to the stranger. "Jack," Ann cried, "I didn't know you had a brother. You have never talked about him."

"A long time ago, we had a big fight," Jack said sadly. "During the war, Dan fought for the North. As a Texan, I fought for the South. But the war is over now. I just thank God that we are both still alive."

Just then, Tommy ran into the room. "Tommy," said Jack, "this is your Uncle Dan." Dan picked up the little boy and gave him a warm hug.

After lunch, Jack and Dan went for a walk. The rain had finally stopped. Dan turned to his brother. "There is something I should tell you," he said. "There are some men looking for me. Back in Deadwood, after the war, I got into a fight over a woman. I killed a man, Jack. If her brothers find me, they'll kill me.

"I've been hiding in caves and moving from town to town. If I work to make some money, I don't use my own name. I've been trying to get to Mexico, but maybe they'll even follow me there. What can I do? Will you help me?"

"I don't know," said Jack. "I have a family to think about now, you know. I have an Indian friend named Gray Hawk. He helped me when Molly was killed and Tommy was lost. Maybe he could help you too, Dan. I could go and talk to him tomorrow."

Chapter 5

Jack began to think about what Dan told him. His brother had killed a man! Jack was the sheriff now. How could he help his brother run from the law? "Dan," he said, "you know I'm the sheriff here. Before I help you, you'll have to tell me how this happened."

Dan sat on a tree stump. "You

know how bad it was in the war, Jack," he said. "I was in battles where you could walk across the field and never step on the ground. There were that many dead bodies. When the war was over, I'd think about all my dead friends and drink. A lot. I'm not saying that it was right. I'm saying that it's what I did.

"Then, in Deadwood, I met a woman. Her name was Sarah. She was sad because the man she planned to marry had been killed in the war. We had a lot in common. I'm not sure I loved her, but we were both lonely. We spent a lot of time together. Sarah's brothers didn't like me because I was drinking too much. They told me to get out of town. I didn't care. I kept seeing her.

"Then, one night, as I left Sarah's house, her brothers attacked me. There were three of them. It was dark, and they were armed. I was drunk, but I went for my gun and shot at them. I hit one of the men. The other two stayed to help him.

"I ran to a friend's home and hid. When I heard that the man had died, I got a horse and rode away. But Sarah's brothers came after me later. They have been chasing me ever since. They'll never rest until I'm dead, Jack."

Chapter 6

Jack was quiet for a moment. "If you killed the man in self-defense, you won't be hanged," Jack said. "It sounds like you had no choice."

"But it's just my word against theirs," said Dan. "And there are two of them backing each other up. Even so, I'm not as afraid of the judge as I am of Sarah's brothers. Even if the judge lets me go, they'll still come after me. I'll never be free!" cried Dan.

"This is hopeless," Dan continued. "It was wrong of me to put you and your family in danger. I'm sorry, Jack. I'll leave tonight. It's best if I ride in the dark. I'm used to it."

Jack leaned against a tree. He felt sorry for his brother. Dan looked so old and tired. Jack thought back to when they were boys. They were so close as they grew up. And Jack was the only family Dan had left.

"No," Jack said at last, "don't

give up. I'll go to Gray Hawk. Maybe he can think of a way to help you."

Dan stayed with his brother that night. At sunrise, Jack rode out near the river where Chief Gray Hawk and his family were now. The Indians often moved their camp to be near the animals they were hunting.

Jack and Gray Hawk talked for a long time. "My brother is not at peace," said Jack. "When he sleeps, he dreams of what he saw during the war. He drinks too much whiskey, and now he's killed a man. That man's brothers are looking for Dan. If they find him, they will kill him. Can you help us?"

"If he stays with you, your family is in great danger," said Gray Hawk. "Bring Dan to us. We move often, and those men won't think of looking for him at an Indian camp."

"Thank you," said Jack. "Once again you are a friend to me and my family, Gray Hawk."

Chapter 7

For weeks, Dan lived with Gray Hawk's people. He learned many things. The Indians taught him to forgive the people who had hurt him. He even forgave himself for the mistakes he made in his life. He was happy. And he looked forward to the future.

The Indians treated him as part

of their family. They called him "Running Deer." He learned to love and respect the land they called home. Dan hunted only the animals he needed for food and clothing. Before eating meat, he thanked the animal that lost its life.

Running Deer made many friends. He began spending time with a pretty Indian woman named Robin Song. Their lives were different in many ways. Robin Song was bright and curious. She loved to hear Dan talk about his life.

The Indians saw the changes in Dan. They were pleased to

welcome him into their family. They invited him to take part in an annual dance. They ate fried bread and corn. They baked tamales in corn husks and drank peach tea.

Jack, Ann, and Tommy came to the dance. They met Robin Song and her family. Everyone danced, ate, and had fun.

Jack thanked Gray Hawk for helping his brother. He was glad to see Dan looking so happy. Behind his smile, though, Dan knew he had not seen the last of Sarah's brothers.

Chapter 8

One summer night, Running Deer and Robin Song sat by a small fire. They were holding hands and telling stories. Suddenly Jack rode into camp.

"Dan," he yelled, "you must go right away! Sarah's brothers are in town. They're looking for you."

Dan hadn't thought about

Sarah's brothers in a long time. He loved Robin Song and her family. Those men were part of his old life. But Jack was right. Dan was in danger and so was anyone around him. He could not put his new family at risk.

"I have to go now," he said to Robin Song, kissing her. "I will come back to you."

"No," cried Robin Song. "You are one of us now. Run to the tepee and stay there until I call for you."

"You'd better make up your mind," Jack said. "I hear horses coming."

"I should stand and fight like a man," said Dan.

"Go NOW!" Robin Song yelled, and Dan obeyed her. "I will go and get the chief," she said to Jack. "He'll know what to do."

Chief Gray Hawk came just as two men rode up. The men got off their horses and walked over to Jack and the Indians.

"We're looking for Dan Sloan," one of them said. "We heard he was here. Don't make this hard. Turn him over to us and we'll leave you alone. Don't try to help him get away."

The chief walked slowly toward the men. He was tall, with wise eyes and a powerful voice. "We live here in peace with the white men," he said. "We have no fight with you. Why do you want Dan Sloan?"

"Back in Deadwood, we warned him to stay away from our sister, Sarah, but he didn't. We went after him for Sarah's sake," said one of the men. "And Dan Sloan killed our brother."

"Now he must pay for what he did," said the other brother. "Turn him over to us, and by sunup this will all be over." In his hands was a long rope tied into a noose.

Chapter 9

"There is no Dan Sloan here," said Gray Hawk. "He is Running Deer now. And he is one of us. To kill him you will have to fight all of us!"

Just then Running Deer came out of the tepee. "Here I am," he said. "I don't fear you now. I'm sorry I killed your brother.

"That was a night filled with hate and killing. I have learned a better way to live. Can you forgive me and leave me in peace?"

Sarah's brothers looked at the man they had hated for so long. "You think that we can just forgive you and ride away? You must be crazy!" said one brother.

"I've still got the rope," said the other. "I'll see you swing from it before those Indians catch me!"

Jack Sloan walked to the men. "I'm Sheriff Jack Sloan," he said. "I hoped that this could be settled without anyone going to jail."

"Sloan, huh?" said the man with the rope. "He's your brother? You need to take your brother to jail. He is a cold-blooded killer."

"What if we get a judge and have a trial?" asked Jack.

"In your town? You know how it would come out. I say we hang Dan Sloan now!" said Sarah's brother.

"No," said Jack. "We'll have the trial in Deadwood, where the shooting took place. Now, to be fair, I will take my brother to jail. He will stay there until the trial starts."

Chapter 10

The judge was a big man with a white beard. He looked very wise. Jack looked at him and then at Dan. He hoped the judge was fair as well as wise.

No one saw Dan shoot Sarah's brother. So first, Dan told his side of the story to the judge. Then Sarah's brothers told their side of the story. The judge bent toward the men to hear them well.

After everyone had their say, the judge left the room. Some other men went outside to smoke. There was very little talking. Everyone knew that a man could die. And many of those in court knew how hard it had been for Jack to arrest his own brother.

Robin Song stood in the back of the room. Her eyes were filled with tears.

After almost two hours, the judge came back. Everyone sat down in the courtroom. The judge said, "I find Dan Sloan not guilty of murder. I believe that he used his gun only to defend himself."

The judge looked at Dan. "You are free to go, Mr. Sloan," he said. "It's good that you have changed your ways. Now stay away from Deadwood, and keep out of trouble."

Robin Song ran to Dan and put her arms around him.

Jack walked Sarah's brothers out of the courtroom. "We need to talk," Jack said.

Chapter 11

Sarah's brothers went back to Jack's office to talk. They were angry. "Will you be able to let go of your anger now that the trial is over?" asked Jack.

"Well, we know you're happy," said one of the men. "Your brother gets to go free. But our brother is still dead!"

"Look," Jack said. "We all have to live with what the judge said. If you keep after Dan, it won't bring your brother back. Dan feels sorry about this. If he could undo the killing, he would. He doesn't want to run anymore." Jack looked outside to where Dan stood with Robin Song.

"Dan is not the same man he was when he killed your brother. If he can change, can't you?" asked Jack.

"Well, uh," said one of the brothers, "you're asking for something big here, Sheriff. We really miss our brother."

"I'm not saying that you have

to be friends. I'm just asking you to go home and get on with your lives," said Jack. "Dan is a free man now. If you kill him, you will hang."

"We have been away from home a long time," said Sarah's brother. "We do have work to catch up on."

"OK, we'll go home," the other brother said. "We aren't happy about this, but we'll try to live with it."

Dan turned to the men as they walked out with Jack. "I want you to know how sorry I am," he said.

"The sheriff says that you're a

new man, Dan Sloan. I hope that we never see you near our sister again." With that, the brothers rode off.

Dan turned to Robin Song. "I'm a free man now. Will you marry me?" he asked.

"You won't be free for long, Running Deer," she smiled. "Now you belong to me. Let's go tell my family the good news."

Chapter 12

Jack wanted to thank Gray Hawk for his help. So Robin Song, Dan, and Jack rode toward the Indian camp. Soon they saw red and gray in the western sky. "Is that the sun setting?" asked Dan.

"No," said Jack. "It looks like a range fire. Nate Miller lives out there. Let's see if he needs help."

Jack could see clouds of black smoke now. "I'd hate to see Nate lose everything in a fire," he said.

"I'll go see if Gray Hawk can help," said Robin Song. "You go on ahead. It looks like Nate will need all the help he can get."

As Robin Song rode off, Jack and Dan saw lots of cattle heading their way. "Stampede!" cried Dan.

"Look," Jack yelled. "Men on horses, too." At first, Jack and Dan thought that the horsemen were Nate's ranch hands trying to stop the stampede. But soon, they could see that something else was going on.

The horsemen wore rags over their faces and carried guns. They looked like cattle rustlers! Maybe they set the fire so they could run off with Nate's cattle! The cattle thundered by in a great cloud of dust. The armed men followed.

Nate and his ranch hands soon came along. Jack and Dan went after them. But the cattle were scared, and the rustlers were fast on their horses. To make things worse, the fire was getting closer, filling the air with smoke.

Jack choked, and dust made it hard to see. He was riding as fast as his horse would go.

Dan looked back. "The fire is

gaining on us, Jack. Let's split up. It looks like Nate is trying to trap the cattle in the canyon. If we help, we'll have them for sure."

"I'm with you," yelled Jack. He rode to the other side of the running cattle to help herd them toward Buffalo Canyon. Just then, there were shouts and cries as Gray Hawk's people joined them. They could see what the men were doing. They helped surround the herd.

The cattle rustlers fired at them, but didn't hit anyone. It was hard to see anything with all the smoke and dust.

Chapter 13

Once Nate's cattle were safe in Buffalo Canyon, Jack and Dan stopped to rest. Their eyes and noses still burned from the smoke. Gray Hawk rode over to them. "I'm sure I've seen one of those cattle rustlers before," he said. "I think he's a hired gun."

"Let's talk to Nate and see how

the fire started," said Jack. "Maybe we can find out who's behind all this."

They found Nate and his men counting cattle. Nate looked up. "Thanks to all you guys for helping me." Nate looked very tired. His face was black with smoke, and his shirt was wet with sweat. "It's no use trying to save the house," he added. "It's already gone."

"How did the fire start?" asked Jack.

"I think I know," said Nate. "When I first came out here, I just claimed that land. We all did it that way. I let the Indians hunt there, so I had no trouble. I bought cattle, grew corn, and built the house and barns. Now, the government is getting strict about land grants. Rich men want to buy up all the land around here.

"I paid the Indians some gold, but we never wrote anything down. We just shook hands. Now, a man named Carter is claiming most of my land. I think he hired those men to burn my home and fields and steal my cattle."

Chapter 14

As the men rested their horses in Buffalo Canyon, it began to rain. "This should put out what's left of the fire," said Jack. "There's a cave nearby where we can sleep tonight. Carter's men did plenty of damage today. I don't think they'll be back. Come on."

The men washed in a creek as

Justice on Horseback

their horses drank. Then they sat around a small fire. Jack turned to Nate. "As sheriff here, maybe I can help you with the land grant office. It's no use putting up a new house and barns until you're sure that you own that land."

"But it *is* my land!" said Nate. "I've worked hard there for years! All Carter did was ride west and file papers. He never worked the fields in the hot sun."

"The law's the law," said Jack. "And we have to live with it. Do you want to keep fighting with Carter and whoever comes after him? Or do you want to work this out legally, once and for all?

"In the morning, I'll get some men to help me look for the outlaws who started the fire," said Jack. "Even if it turns out that you don't own the land, the cattle are still yours. And I can put those men in jail for running them off.

"We'll leave someone here to watch your cattle. But I want you and Dan to go to the land office and check on the paperwork for your land. You need to find out how much of that land you really own."

"I'll tell you what I own. I own all of it!" shouted Nate.

Chapter 15

Jack, Dan, and Nate started out at sunup. Jack, Gray Hawk, and two other Indians went to look for the men who set the fire. Dan and Nate headed for the land office, which was a good day's trip away.

Nate looked back at his charred land. "I worked so hard. Why doesn't Carter find his own land?"

"More and more people are heading west," said Dan. "This is a good place to begin again. Some people lost everything in the war. Here they can buy acres of land for very little money."

"They can't take my land!" said Nate. "I want what's mine."

"Things are changing fast," said Dan. "Soon the train will go from Boston to Oregon. We used to wait weeks for the mail. Now with the telegraph, we can get messages the same day!"

"Well, *I* want a message that says I own my land," said Nate.

Chapter 16

The land office was busy. Men stood in line with papers and maps in their hands. Nate and Dan were the only ones without papers.

Finally Nate's turn came. "A man named Carter says he owns most of my ranch," said Nate. "He burned my house and ran off my cattle. I need proof I own my land."

The tall bald man looked up at Nate. "Did you ever file an official land claim?" he asked.

"Why?" asked Nate. "This was years before the war. There was no government office here. I got that land from the Indians. I traded them gold and crops. Everyone was happy up till now."

"You should have filed a claim with the government right after the war ended," said the clerk.

"What about homesteader's rights?" asked Dan.

"Sorry," said the clerk. "You

still need a claim. Go home and make a map of your land. Maybe you can still claim the rest of it."

Nate walked slowly out of the office. "I'm not even sure where my land ends," he said.

"Stay here," said Dan. He went back into the office. He drew a copy of the map on the wall. It showed where land claims had already been filed. When he came back out, he showed Nate the map.

"There's good land just south of yours," Dan said. "If you add that to what Carter didn't get, it will be the same size your ranch was."

"I still have to pay for land I already own!" said Nate.

"Yes," said Dan, "but you'll have proof you own that land."

"What if they change the rules again?" asked Nate.

"You'll have to take that chance," said Dan. "If you don't file now, you won't have any land left to claim."

Nate thanked Dan for the map. He took it back inside and got in line. In the back of his mind, Dan was dreaming of filing his own claim. He could not wait to settle down with Robin Song.

Chapter 17

While Nate and Dan were at the land office, Jack, Gray Hawk, and some others rode after the rustlers. "Look for smoke or tracks," said Jack. "They can't be far away."

One of the Indians held up his hand, and the men stopped their horses. He pointed toward the bottom of a nearby hill. Three men were packing their saddlebags. When one of them saw Jack and his friends, he grabbed a rifle.

Gray Hawk was faster. A gunfight began. Many shots were fired. Suddenly it was very quiet.

"It's over," said Jack. One man was walking toward him with both hands up. The other two were on the ground. One wasn't moving.

Jack and Gray Hawk were all right. One Indian was shot. Gray Hawk made sure he was OK.

Jack put handcuffs on the outlaw who turned himself in. Then he checked on the other two.

One was bleeding, but he'd live. The other was dead. Jack tied the outlaws onto horses.

The ride home was long and quiet. A doctor in town tended the wounded man. Then Jack locked both outlaws in jail. He asked why they set the fire and stole the cows.

The men said Carter paid them to scare Nate. "You two will have a fair trial," Jack told them. "But look at the price your friend paid for a little gold!"

Jack said to Gray Hawk, "This won't be over until I find Carter."

Chapter 18

The next day, Nate and Dan were back in town. They told Jack what happened at the land office.

"Two of Carter's men are in jail," said Jack. "Another man is dead. But I still want to find Carter. He hired those men, and he'll have to answer to me."

"If Carter goes to jail, he won't

need my land," Nate said with a grim smile.

"We have to find him first," said Jack. "So let's get going."

Jack, Dan, and Nate spent the day asking everyone in town about Carter. Before long, Jack heard about a rich man who was staying at the boarding house.

The three men rushed over to the boarding house. A large man in a new black suit and fancy boots was eating a big dinner. Carter had a round face with mean eyes. He asked, "You men here for a meal?"

"No, we're here to see you,"

Jack replied. "I'm Sheriff Jack Sloan. This is my brother, Dan. And this is Nate Miller. It was his cattle your men tried to steal."

"Why, I've only been here a few days," said Carter. "I came here to file a land claim. Now I'm looking for cattle and horses for my new ranch." Carter smiled at Nate. "Too bad someone burned your ranch and stole your cattle," he said.

Jack chuckled. "I didn't say anything about a fire," he said. "Besides, I have two men in the jail who told me that you paid them to scare off Nate. Now come with me, Mr. Carter."

Justice on Horseback

Carter's eyes glowed with anger. "I paid good money for that land. It's mine. If I want to burn it, you can't stop me!" Carter stood up, pounding his fist on the table.

"Oh yes I can," Jack said. "Those cattle belong to Nate. And out here, cattle rustling is a crime."

Carter's face turned beet red. "I didn't rustle any cattle." Sweat poured down his face. Then he grabbed his chest and slid to the floor. His eyes stared up blankly.

"Get the doctor!" Jack yelled.

"Too late," said Dan. His hand was on Carter's unmoving chest.

Chapter 19

Life slowly returned to normal over the next month. With Carter dead, Nate got to keep his ranch. He also claimed the extra land to the south. Jack and Dan helped him put up a new house and barns. Nate was glad to be home again before cold weather came.

The crisp fall days meant

Justice on Horseback

harvest celebrations for the Indians. Dan and Robin Song decided it was the perfect time for a wedding. Jack, his family, and many friends joined Gray Hawk's clan for the party. They all had many reasons to be happy.

"I'm glad that my brother and I are close again," Jack said. "And now that he has a wife, he can start his own family. I hope he is as happy as I am."

"Yes," Ann replied softly. "Family is so important. I want Dan to know the kind of happiness we share. And soon we'll have a new little member of our family to love."

"Do you mean . . . ?" asked Jack.

"I think Tommy would like a little brother or sister, don't you?" asked Ann with a smile.

"I didn't think I could ever be happier," said Jack. "But now I know that anything is possible."